Written and illustrated by Jenny Jiang

JUST LIKE FLOWERS

Dedicated to my friends and family,
who taught me that every seed blossoms into its own
unique flower

Just Like Flowers
Text and illustrations copyright © 2021 by Jenny Jiang
All rights reserved. No part of this book may be used or reproduced in any manner whatsoever without written permission except in the case of brief quotations embedded in critical articles or reviews.
For more information, contact:
Jenny Jiang at jennyjiang6863@gmail.com
Written and illustrated by Jenny Jiang
ISBN: 9781087926391
10 9 8 7 6 5 4 3 2 1
First edition, 2021

Julia was painting herself in her art class.
 "It's now time to paint my hair," said Julia. She went to grab a purple paint bottle, but she did not have that color.

When she looked around her class, Julia saw that no one was using purple paint.

They were instead using red, blue, and black paint . . .

. . . but not purple paint.

"What's wrong, Julia?" Ms. Ross asked when she noticed Julia had stopped painting.

Julia replied, "Why am I the only person who has purple hair?" She felt upset that no one else needed purple paint.

Ms. Ross smiled and told her, "You may look different, but that's what makes you special! Think about all of our differences as the different flowers in a garden."

Ms. Ross went to the nearest planter box and picked up two flowers. One flower was a golden yellow tulip, and the other one was a white calla lily.

"Look at these flowers, Julia. Which color do you think is prettier?"

Julia loved the yellow petals, but she also enjoyed the white petals. "I can't choose! These flowers are so pretty."

"Exactly! Both colors are wonderful. Now, look at you and Layla. Her skin is the color of a pearl. Your skin is the color of honey. Your skin colors are different but still look beautiful on each of you."

Julia noticed how even though the flowers were different colors, both the flowers were still lovely — just like her and Layla!

Ms. Ross picked up two new flowers and asked, "What's the difference between these?"

Julia noticed how one flower had a round shape, and the other flower was more narrow.

"Well, Ms. Ross, one is shaped like a circle, and the other is shaped like a rectangle."

"Perfect!" Ms. Ross said. "Look at how both of these flowers are pleasing even though they're shaped differently. This is like you and Gabriel. You two have different body types, but that's what makes both of you uniquely beautiful."

Julia was starting to understand! The differences in flowers were like the differences between her and her classmates.

Julia picked two flowers on her own. One flower was the length of her arm, while the other one was the length of her hand.

"Ms. Ross, I have a tall and short flower, and they're both amazing!"

Ms. Ross nodded. "You and Amala are different heights, just like these flowers."

"I've always wanted to be a little taller, but being short is cool too! I'm like a shorter flower." Julia added.

Ms. Ross grabbed all the flowers around her and gave them to Julia. "Look at this bouquet."

"What does the word 'bouquet' mean?" Julia asked.

"A bouquet means a group of flowers. What would the bouquet look like with only one type of flower?"

Julia imagined a bouquet of only roses. The bouquet was a little boring because each flower looked the same. The vibrant bouquet caught more of her attention from all of the unique flowers.

"Each flower is really different, which makes this bouquet exciting. This is like our own beauty!" Ms. Ross explained.

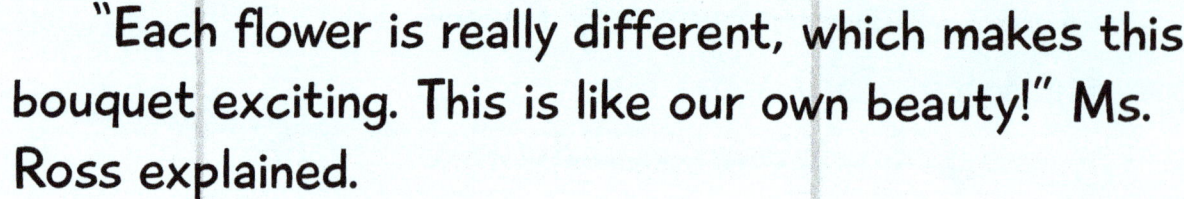

"Every person looks different, just like these flowers. We should love these traits that make us, us. So don't be sad that you're the only one with purple hair, Julia. That's what makes you your own special flower in our bouquet."

Julia looked around. Everyone had a different skin color, body shape, and height.

"And just like every flower, each of my friends is beautiful!" Julia cheered.

"Exactly!" Ms. Ross agreed and asked Julia if she wanted a hug.
"Yes, I'm so happy I learned this!"

"But wait!" Julia shouted, "What about my painting? I still don't have any purple paint."

Julia loved Amala's idea, so she quickly went to work. She got all their paint bottles and started mixing the red, blue, and black paint. Slowly, the paint formed a dark purple color.

The new paint was a perfect match for Julia's hair. "This purple is perfect!" She grabbed her paintbrush and finished her painting. Her artwork now looked like herself. . .

. . . but the painting was missing one last thing.

Julia dipped her paintbrush in red, blue, and black paint. When she finished, everyone leaned in to look.

Her painting had red, blue, and black flowers! And each flower had a different color, shape, and height.

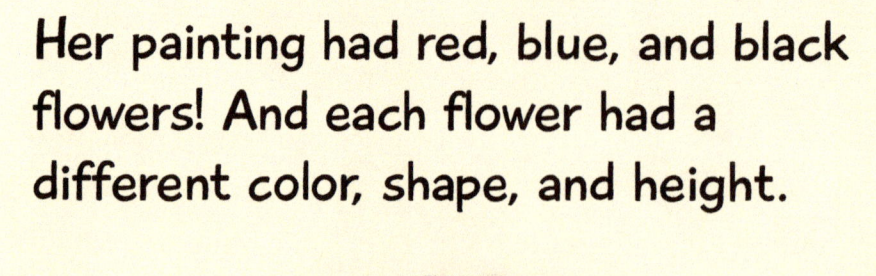

Ms. Ross smiled. "What a beautiful bouquet of flowers!"

CPSIA information can be obtained
at www.ICGtesting.com
Printed in the USA
LVHW070035160322
713573LV00002B/96